圣诞花
CHRISTMAS BLOSSOMS

Sursum Corda !

Priscilla Smith McCaffrey

CHRISTMAS
Blossoms

PRISCILLA SMITH MCCAFFREY

Illustrations by Gwyneth Thompson-Briggs

SOPHIA INSTITUTE PRESS

Manchester, New Hampshire

Sophia Institute Press

Box 5284, Manchester, NH 03108

1-800-888-9344

www.SophiaInstitute.com

Sophia Institute Press® is a registered trademark of Sophia Institute.

paperback ISBN 978-1-64413-578-5

ebook ISBN 978-1-64413-579-2

Library of Congress Control Number: 2021943479

First printing

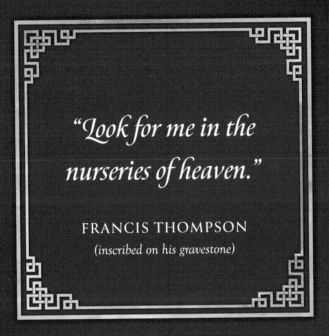

"*Look for me in the nurseries of heaven.*"

FRANCIS THOMPSON
(inscribed on his gravestone)

INTRODUCTION

Dear Friends,

    Christmas Blossoms is about a Chinese artisan who has lived in my imagination for many years. His name is Zhang Jian. As a boy, he knew the Catholic Church in China, up until the Revolution of 1949, when the faithful were targeted and his family was cruelly split apart. His lifelong work is painting the inside of glass ornaments, mostly for Christmas. He has much to say to his fellow artists about the sights and smells of Christmas. In this story, Jian is an old man in love with the memory of his family during that holy season. He comes to realize that he has one last ornament to make so the world understands who he is—who we all are—before the Christ Child.

Jian was born in 1940 and died at around the age of seventy-five. The Communist Revolution overturned the old order when he was nine. Most missionaries were sent away or died with their flocks. Families were broken up and often lost forever in the turmoil, some due to the chaos, others due to the policies of the Government Central Planning Committee. Gradually it was established that anything strictly from the West was either decadent—like capitalism—or subversive, like Christianity. In order to "purify" China of these foreign influences, a grim effort known as the Cultural Revolution took place from 1966 to 1976. Many noble people suffered and died in the purge, and those who survived lived in terror of the Red Guards. Not just foreign influences but China's own traditions were suspect and therefore discarded in favor of the new ideology, Maoism. The feared Chinese Red Guards were often young people schooled to make one group hate another. They violated the lives and peaceful ways of ordinary people. Mao caused a great famine with his failed "Great Leap Forward" to industrialize the country and, with three decades of purges, caused the unnatural deaths of more than sixty-five million people. And sadly, there was a major earthquake in the Hebei province in 1976 that killed at least three hundred thousand people.

So, you see, Jian's China has a sad history.

At the time of my story, some churches have been allowed to open again. Men and women are using their talents to start successful businesses. Talent abounds, and Chinese citizens are looking for reasons to hope.

But the winds of tolerance can suddenly change, so Jian must stay ever alert to what is permissible and what is not. Freedom of religion does not exist, and family size is under tight state control. In 2021, it was decided that women may have three children, given how disastrous the previous one- and two-child policies were for societal growth and maintenance.

Let us pray for the suffering Church in China and for all Chinese men and women of good will.

God, graciously hear us!

圣诞快乐
MERRY CHRISTMAS!
Priscilla Smith McCaffrey

Zhang Jian was a master artist of interior glass painting, in the employ of the Fulida Company, in the city of Tianjin, in the province of Hebei, in the country of China.

Or, at least, he had been for many years. His worthy hands could no longer hold the fine brushes to make the delicate strokes inside snuff bottles, glass balls, and vases.

His hands now were only good for rough brooms and cleaning towels. He could have lived humbly on his pension, but there was no one home to share his tea, and the days were long.

Others of his skill became teachers of the traditional handicraft. But Zhang Jian could not find the words to instruct. Directions became a tangle in his head, and he would take up the students' time talking, talking, talking about what he was painting, but never how. He had come by his own skill naturally; he had not been taught and could not understand how to offer advice.

Jian became a part of modern factory life, even in old age. Lin Renshu, the floor supervisor of Christmas ornaments, liked to have him around. When Jian went to the artists' tables to clean brushes and pots, he offered more than a nod and fresh paint. Renshu and Jian had worked together for many years. They were old men now, comfortable in each other's presence. Renshu had always liked Jian's paintings because they made his shop famous, and that brought contracts. Jian had always thought Renshu very clever, keeping the shop opened for so many years.

Renshu did not know what Jian said to the other employees. He just knew that Jian made them cheerful or more careful with their work. The work of the floor was to fill thousands of orders for painted Christmas tree ornaments.

In the present days, the shop was very busy. Christmas had come back to China!

喜悦

In his tiny apartment, Jian thought about the Christmases of his boyhood. He had been born into a Catholic family in this province in 1940. He had known Christmas as Chinese Catholics had honored the day.

Jian thought of his mother and his venerable father greeting the priests at the door after Midnight Mass. On those nights, the priests carried lanterns and sang Western carols outside the Zhang home, and they would not be let in until they sang the Chinese version of "Jingle Bells." Everybody roared at their ridiculous accent.

Fr. LeBeque once poured golden liquid from a jug onto the snow, and the children ran to pick up the frozen molasses treats formed into extended dragons. Jian remembered several Christmas Eves, which to his mind were perfection, celebrated in the warm splendor of the home they shared with many relatives. It had all become an untouched memory, an idyllic image in a snow globe. The world outside was cold and crisp and expectant. Their home was warm and rich in color, fragrance, and words of cheer and kindness.

On those nights, the priests carried lanterns and sang Western carols outside the Zhang home, and they would not be let in until they sang the Chinese version of "Jingle Bells."

In 1949, revolution engulfed China. Ashen clouds smothered his snow-globe world. There was no longer soft lantern light to illumine the pilgrims' path, and there were no parents to welcome carolers transported from the West to bring good news of "the Orient from on High."

Jian had been cruelly separated from the people of his village after his parents were taken. There were so many sad and vague memories. He had only told his wife some of these, as if in duty to his parents. There was also a little brother and sister. These, too, he would give some honor to by remembering them. But it was all wrapped in days of pain. He wanted to keep alive their memories; he wanted to keep his happy family in the snow globe. The Central Planning Committee might have separated him from them forever, but it could not separate him from their memory.

When he turned to thoughts of his family, it was always Christmas Eve. His family meant Christmas to him, and Christmas meant his family.

So, in the factory, when Shi Zhenzhen and Cai Ru turned to him with their brushes, Jian would tell them about the flavors, scents, and shadows of Advent; the dark days of expectation; and the happy moods of Christmas. They would know what to do, for they understood color and mood, not just color and symbol.

He explained this to his beloved wife, Nuo. She was a fine painter, who used the traditional colors of Chinese festivals in her work. Her ornaments were always cheerful. He showed her that more could be said, more moods could be created, using shades of color. She began to see and loved him for his many shades of understanding. His art began to color her own perspective of Christmas; there was more compassion in his way of thinking.

Jian thought about the many ways the Party had presented Christmas. Today, it was no longer an evil cult; it had become business.

宁静

Renshu and Jian had lived through the days when Christmas was officially declared a "decadent season" from the "poisonous West." More than anything, this taught the young Jian how wrong the Planning Committee could be. He knew they had no idea what Christmas truly was.

He tried once to explain Christmas to his boyhood friends when December days came around. "It started with a poor Baby in a manger who came to save us all." But he was smacked by Wang Feng's mother, who said that it was the Party that had come to save the sons and daughters of the new China from living in stalls and using mangers as beds.

Jian remembered the sad days. It was true: the Child in the manger had not kept his parents from being taken away. He had not saved them. Jian knew the Child was the reason his parents were taken away and the priests disappeared. They had chosen the Child and not him. And for many years that had brought him sorrow.

But the seasons passed many times over, and he grew to understand that for his parents to love him truly, they had needed to love that little Child in the manger, for that Child represented the purity of their own children. They chose to stay with Him rather than willingly give their children to Herod's men, who would deform their minds and make them slaves of the state. They would die for Jian's own honor and the honor of his brother and sister. He knew they trusted that the Child in the manger would show the children their own worth.

When he became a man, he decided he, too, would stay with the Child in the manger. So he kept in his pocket a tiny replica of the Christ Child. It had been part of a set his own father had made years earlier. Jian's wife, Nuo, knew that he carried it. She would always check for it before laundering his pants. If he had not removed it, she would take it out and kiss it. She only knew that it meant a love for his father and mother.

When Nuo longed for her own child, she would kiss the little Christ and put Him beneath her pillow at night, returning Him to Jian's pocket in the early morning. He knew she did this but never spoke to her of it. The Christ Child had caused him to lose his parents and had helped him to reestablish their memory; Jian did not want to lose Nuo because of Him, for China had grown very cruel to Christians. In 1966, no Christian was safe from the madness of the Red Guards, who perceived all things

When Nuo longed for her own child, she would kiss the
little Christ and put Him beneath her pillow at night,
returning Him to Jian's pocket in the early morning.

non-Chinese in origin as evil. He could not bear to see his little Jesus tossed into the deep shadows.

He remembered again the story of Herod and the Holy Innocents. When he was young and had lost the instruction of the priests, he had believed the story to be made up, because no one could be so cruel to children. Sadly, over the years, he learned how easy it was for the Red Guards to spread their terror and cruelty. He would not let anything endanger Nuo. He loved his little Jesus, but he knew He was dangerous for her. The figure must be kept in hiding, exiled to his pocket.

The evil days of the persecution passed, but not all evil passed with it. In 1976, there was the worst earthquake recorded in their province, and he lost Nuo and their long-awaited child.

Jian and his tiny Jesus were alone once again.

同情

Renshu remembered those days. For many weeks Jian could not pick up a brush. He would come to his station in the morning and sit and stare, fists clenched, unable to speak. Renshu knew that he suffered deeply from the loss of his wife and son and so gave him little, necessary jobs to keep him moving about. But Jian was like a dead man inside, incapable of thought or self-direction. When the sun shone through the factory window, Renshu would have Jian sit in the sunlight and clean the ornaments. In time, Jian had had enough of so many silly Christmas scenes. He began to take some back to his own station and finish them off. No one complained. Everyone was glad to have him back.

和谐

For thirty years more, Jian worked on Christmas ornaments. He painted snowmen and snowflakes, the coziest of hearth scenes and winter wonderlands—the popular images of the West. He knew Westerners were rich enough to give these as "thoughtful little gifts." Still, it gave him joy to think his work swung from the boughs of evergreens around the world. He imagined the looks on the faces of young girls who received a glass ball with brilliant stallions painted inside, or boys who loved the far seas and held a glass bubble with billowing sails. There might be a grandmother whose gift glistened with the colors of sunrise, or an aged uncle who smiled at a kingfisher catching fire. All things of beauty, all things of serendipity, could be conjured through his brush and take life on the glass surface.

But he loved most of all to paint the Nativity scene. In the early years when Christianity was out of favor, Jian felt self-conscious. He must be perfunctory and paint as if he did not care about the Nativity. He must paint in

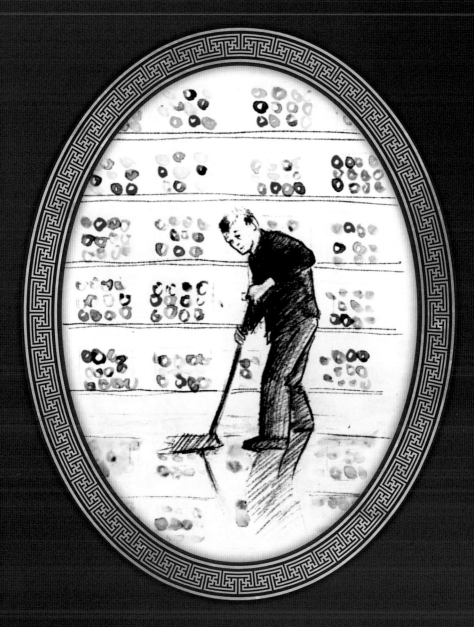

He imagined the looks on the faces of young girls who received
a glass ball with brilliant stallions painted inside, or boys who
loved the far seas and held a glass bubble with billowing sails.

primary colors, a child's palette. This was doubly hard for Jian because the Nativity reminded him of the happy days with his family. These were full-bodied memories of joyous life, and the simple colors deformed that reality. He also knew he must not spend too much time with it. A manger; a woman; and a man with a crook, hand on heart. Straw cast about. A star on high. These were the basic elements.

After a few seasons, he began to paint from his own memories. Renshu easily found buyers for these more sincere works. Jian thought to himself, this is what I would have shown my son, how it was when the priests sang at the tops of their voices, and everyone was in good cheer. He would not forget the splash of lantern light on new-fallen snow. Everything sparkled, and the sparkle was the glory of the Christ Child.

When he painted, he could hear the laughter of the French-Canadian priests and smell the Cognac they shared with his father. He had grown to love these men, strangers to his country now, who had come so far. They had left the comfort of their own people who rejoiced with the yearly Christmas anniversary. Jian knew the Western stories of Santa Claus traveling the world on the Eve of Christmas, but they could not compare to the travels of the men who called them their "brothers in Christ." Every year he understood better what they had sacrificed to bring China the news of the newborn King.

Jian mostly stayed away from the churches as they emerged once again in the '80s. Some were to be honored, and some were not to be regarded at all, for they were sponsored by the government. He wished he could ask his mother and father to tell him what he should do. He did not want to compromise his love for the Christ Child in his pocket through an inauthentic worship nor violate the memories of his dear parents.

The people of the New Religion were kind and worthy, but there were never quiet moments in their churches; so much was missing of venerable tradition, and they never prayed for their dead. He dared not go often, but when he attended the Mass of the Old Rites, he felt he was as close to his parents as he could be. He stood as they had stood, he knelt as they had knelt, he prayed as they prayed, and he bent his head with them in adoration. He was at Mass with them.

美

Jian's pocket Christ was sometimes shared with friends and sent on missions of comfort. Su-Lin, the wife of Shen Ping, had grown sick in her pregnancy. Jian gave the little Jesus to Ping. Chinese always wish "good luck" when sometimes they mean "God bless you." Jian said, "This little Baby will bring you good luck if you simply say, 'Your holy will be done.'" That was as close as Jian could get to the real words. Ping told him he and Su-Lin said it many times each day, and when poor Su-Lin lost her baby, they understood that the Christ Child had made them strong and helped them understand that luck was not as important as the work of Heaven. Once or twice over the years, Jian saw them at Holy Mass. They never spoke of it, and now Su-Lin had twin boys—one pregnancy with two sons! In the days of China's one-child policy, this was considered pure luck!

Even the Central Planning Committee could do nothing about that. Ping and Su-Lin knew their joy was a burden for others to behold. So much luck received; would there be any left for others? That is what some non-Christians would wonder. Jian, Ping, and Su-Lin all knew blessings had no limits.

Another time, Baby Jesus had traveled to the women's hospital with Renshu's daughter-in-law, and she gave birth to a beautiful baby girl, the greatest delight to parents and grandparents. They learned how much a baby can be loved, even if it is not a boy.

And once Baby Jesus had a sad mission. Ming's niece in the countryside had given birth to a third child and could not pay the fines. Ming gave her niece the little Christ Child to hold for six weeks. Her niece was allowed to nurse her infant but then had to give her baby up to the orphanage for adoption. Ming's niece's baby was not given up because she was unwanted; she would be forever loved. With great strength, Ming's niece said she was glad she gave life to this tiny baby, who would bring great happiness to another family.

The baby was her third daughter. Three was an auspicious number and rang in the ear with the same sound as the word "life." She would keep this thought in her heart and confided it to Baby Jesus and her aunt. She said it was a consolation.

圣诞

Two weeks into December, there was always a feeling of relief, because new orders could not be delivered before Christmas. Renshu looked the other way when the workmen stretched at their benches and laughed over their playful creations that no one could sell. These were days when they were allowed to experiment with their art. Many of these objects would end up as gifts to grace the branch of an evergreen, placed in the family home in honor of the "silly" Western holiday of Christmas that had caused their factory to be so famous.

The Avenue of Eternal Peace had flower shops where trees with intact roots might be bought. But mostly the workers of the Fulida Company would buy a branch or two to set on a shelf. They would decorate it with artificial snow and place their glass bubbles along the evergreen, luminous with a string of lights. Even this little bit was magical.

祷告

One frosty evening shortly before Christmas, Jian went to Renshu's apartment for tea. He saw the fine display of light and evergreen and sparkling glass. The ornament in the middle was one of his own Nativity scenes. That was very correct, thought Jian—the Nativity should be central.

Unexpectedly, a word came to Jian that he had not heard for many years: "sacramental." The display reminded him of the side altars he had visited with his grandmother. It was a reminder of heavenly things. Frosty and Santa, delicate snowflakes, a pine wood etched in silver, an egret in a palm tree: all these referenced the Baby in the manger. He did not know quite how to explain this, but it all fit together.

Renshu saw the soft look in the eye of his old comrade. "What are you thinking of, my friend?"

Tonight Jian would not be shy about his past and the days of Christmas. It now seemed silly to be so afraid to talk about a little Jewish family from two thousand years ago. All Chinese knew about the Jewish people.

Renshu brought his friend tea and, out of courtesy, spoke carefully in the old way.

"My Christmas, my family. Its warmth."

Renshu brought his friend tea and, out of courtesy, spoke carefully in the old way. "What is Christmas for the Religion of the Lord of Heaven? Why do you celebrate the birth of a little Jewish boy? Why would Chinese raise Him above their ancestors?"

The painters at Fulida often called upon Jian to explain the significance of Christmas, but each time he presented it as a Western myth. Some of their friends worked in shops that manufactured trinkets for the tourists in Italy and Greece: miniature Parthenons in honor of the Grecian Athena and delicate statues of Venus stepping out of a shell. They made variations of wolves suckling baby boys. Of late, many had been inventive with rosaries for pious fingers as well as fashionistas. These were the trinkets, the charms, the good luck amulets of the West. The East had her own.

It was in this context that Jian explained Christmas. He would tell his fellow artisans, "Christians believe that the one God chose a special people. These were the Jews, the children of Abraham. He promised that they would become great someday under a venerable leader, called the Messiah, but this leader came in disguise, so as to escape the jealousy of powerful men. He was God, but He came as a man. He came one starry night in Bethlehem, two thousand years ago, born in a humble stable. Angels, shepherds, and wise men who knew the stars paid their respects to the newborn. Some called him 'Savior,' others 'King.' He worked miracles and told people how to live wisely."

The rest of the narrative did not sound like a myth, and it disappointed the artists of Fulida that the Messiah told people to love their enemies. They could not understand why the Christians would choose to follow someone, who, though a good man with wise things to say, had died a dishonorable death. This was not the stuff of good myth. It was a story of powerlessness. He had no State to protect Him, and it was His own people who had betrayed Him.

Something was missing from the story. Even when Jian explained that Jesus rose from the dead, they still thought it inconvenient that He then left His followers. Why would the "Savior" leave everyone else in the world to do the work that He Himself could have done? It did not sound like the work of a reasonable God who wanted the world to be better.

Jian would think, but not say aloud, "He did not want the world to be better; He wanted people to be better." Jian was often sorry after he explained these things. He was not successful in making his fellow workers love Jesus the man and Jesus Son of God. But he had succeeded, he thought, in making them love the Baby in the manger; Baby Jesus had brought their shop money and fame. He was good luck.

Tonight he would explain more to Renshu; even if he failed in his explanations, it would bring him joy to talk about the true Christmas story.

"The Baby was 'Emmanuel,' meaning 'God with us.' He brought luck to the people." Then he corrected himself: "No. He brought goodness that He showed before all men. He was God through whom all things were made. A bit more than two thousand years ago, He became man and took the name Jesus, which means 'Savior.' Wise men knew Him as King and humble shepherds recognized Him as a pleasing offering before God the Father."

Renshu did not understand how there could be only one God, if both the Child and the Father were God.

"There is one God, but He is three Persons," Jian began, "the Father, the Son, and the Holy Spirit. You understand how we Chinese love our dragons. Dragons have many meanings. The Christian God has three meanings, or expressions, but each expression is a Person. Each is fully God. One is the Creator, or 'Father.' One is the Creator's 'Word,' or 'Son,' and one is the Love between the Creator and His Son. That is the Holy Spirit."

Renshu could not think too deeply on this, but he could honor it as a Christian mystery. There is always harmony in nature when there is three of something. It is nice to think of the Divine as a harmony and as a holy community without competing gods. He did not quarrel with this concept; a god's nature might well be above his understanding.

"But when the Savior came, why would He hide His power? Why would He come as a little Baby instead of as a conquering warrior who would destroy the landowners and imperialists?" (He dared not say revolutionaries.)

"I cannot say. But He wanted us to be like Him, I think. We cannot be powerful like a god, but we can be good. He came as a poor Baby, showing Himself even poorer than His family really was. He was of a peasant family but born in a stable. His father Joseph had a trade. Even our farmers do not give birth in the stalls of animals. And yet our artists at Fulida understand the charm of His birth. You know well the success of our artists who are not Christian yet love this image of peace and love. The West has given us this image of peace and love, and we make our money from it."

"It is an enchantment."

Jian laughed softly. "The West has very few enchantments for us, but this, I think, is their greatest, and it is for all. Poor people as well as rich buy our ornaments. He came to save the landowners, too."

"From whom does He save the landowners?"

"I don't know. Perhaps from themselves."

"A man, a woman, and their baby," Jian continued, as he stood up and walked toward the shelf. "It's a simple image drawn from the countryside on a starry night. There are shepherds. All is calm. All is in harmony. Even the ox and the ass nod their assent."

Jian selected one of the ornaments from Renshu's display. It did not have pictures but had the Chinese characters for harmony and calm scripted in black and gold.

He is Héping 和平

Together they meant peace. He recognized his own work of many years ago. He had made the ornament for Renshu in the slow days before the Christian Christmas.

"It seems to be in the right place since your Christmas is a day of peace," Renshu commented.

"Yes, but there is more. In these strokes are the lessons of the God-man Jesus, who came down from Heaven to die in our place for our sins and who continues to commune with us under a common appearance until we can be happy with Him in Heaven." He did not expect Renshu to follow his meditation, but this lesson had been a happy discovery for him, and it warmed him to consider it now and to think that Renshu was harboring a very Catholic symbol.

He touched the first character, which was really made of two characters set close together. He first pointed out what they both knew. One character stood for "grain," and the other for "mouth." Together they meant "harmony." Certainly, the wise men who devised these strokes long ago understood that when people were fed, there would be harmony among them. The harmony was not simply satisfaction; it was a kind of good will among men.

The other character represented calm. It bore a slight resemblance to a scale. All is just and right when the scale is in balance. But Jian had rendered the scale as a black cross finished by gold strokes.

"Here is the lesson," he said. "Our two Chinese characters you see together mean 'peace.' A Catholic can look at these and say that he finds his peace by partaking in the Body and Blood of Jesus, who comes to feed our souls, for He is the Bread of Life. He satisfies our open mouths with the finest wheat. He gives life to our souls and nourishes them."

And then Jian traced the next character, for "calm." "You see, I have emphasized the Cross in this character by making it black. The black and gold together render the scale of justice. But how are we to become just before the God of all the living? We who have failed so many times and disgraced ourselves and hurt others? He who is the Bread of Life first offered Himself up to the ignominy of the Cross. He has made it possible for us to become right with God the Father. He took on the shame and asks that we follow Him. His way is peace, and He gives Himself to us as food for the journey. He is *Héping*." He is Peace.

Was this too much for Renshu, wondered Jian. But Renshu only said with a gentle laugh, "Whenever you talk about Jesus, you also talk about food. You even put Him in a manger, a feeding trough for animals!" Renshu did not want to hurt his friend. He knew the Christians had suffered for their Faith, and he liked how their God was only good. Theirs was not a capricious god. So he added cheerfully, "You must see that I am invited to your banquet when you no longer have to think of that cross."

Jian smiled and put the ornament of peace back, close to the Nativity scene. The gold strokes made the black cross look victorious. Jian knew Chinese sometimes understood the compassionate god as the one who knows you suffer and suffers with you but is powerless before the fates. Jian liked the simple way of the Christian God; He had suffered once, for all. His suffering had done something. Christ had made it possible for Jian to become a child of God through the waters of Baptism. The Christian God suffers no more but is with you as you suffer. He draws men to take up their cross, for it has great meaning, and He gives them the grace to bear it. This Jian knew was true. The suffering would continue, but Jian was so close to life's end that he knew there would be an unfolding of the mystery of suffering, and all would be well. Harmony, calm, balance, peace. The ancients had known what peace and justice looked like. What a grace, Jian thought.

Jian felt lighthearted when he left his friend. He had spoken more of Jesus to Renshu than he ever had to anyone. It so cheered him that he knew nothing could prevent him from attending Christmas Mass that year.

The bishop at St. Joseph's, he found out, was in good standing with the old Fathers as well as the government. This caused Jian some confusion, but he knew he must take advantage of this opportunity. The winds of tolerance would shift, no doubt, but for now, he was free to attend the Mass of the Nativity.

星

The first problem to address was the matter of Confession. He was surprised to find out how easy this was to tend to. Confession times were publicly announced, and Jian found himself in line just two days before Christmas.

All his sins over the years, his disloyalties, his acts of cowardice, floated up in the shadow of the confessional and popped before him like little bubbles. Gone more neatly than a bauble dropped to the concrete floor of the Fulida shop. They were no more. The words of the priest were of pure comfort. He said that surely an old man who had held to the Faith for so many decades and through so many hardships was deeply loved by God. Zhang Jian left the church with a heart filled with joy. He would never again miss Christmas Mass.

Lucky for Jian, Christmas that year fell on his day off. That meant he could take his old bones to Midnight Mass.

儿童

It was a rare winter night with the moon bright. Stars twinkled overhead. (Yes, indeed they twinkled.) The chill breeze carried the scent of snow despite the clear night. Jian walked confidently up the steps to the Cathedral of St. Joseph, guardian of families. He had climbed these steps as a happy boy on Christmas Eve with his hand in his father's. Jian was caught up in the mystery and enchantment of the night even before he entered the church.

He reminded himself that he was not in his snow globe, a glass bubble with the perfections of all Christmases captured within. The reality was far better. The altar was bedecked with the national flower, so precious to the eye and heart of the ancients. On the pruned and pendulous branches of a plum tree, blossoms flowered against the snowy linens.

He offered a little prayer as he knelt down, that he be inspired to make an offering pleasing to the Christ Child.

记忆

He came back from Communion with deep repose and calm. He had been truly fed; the open mouth in harmony was satisfied with the finest wheat. He was at peace. There was pain in his old, stiff knees, but not the kind of pain that could distract from what he was at that moment, an old man, suffering, hurting with the pain, but knowing that he was loved.

A bit of cool air wafted overhead, and the people stirred. He looked at the children in the pew ahead. They had been well behaved, sleeping through much of the Mass, as his little sister had done. The tiny boy moved a miniature figure across the pew. The boy's sister, sitting on the kneeler beside him, had her own figure. His was Joseph; hers was Mary. They processed together and rested at a knot in the plank, where Mary bent over to kiss an imaginary Baby. Jian reached into his pocket and pulled out his Baby Jesus. The resemblance to the children's figures was remarkable—the proportions perfect, as if they had been crafted by the same artist. Had his heart not been so full, he could not have parted with his lifelong companion. He kissed Baby Jesus as he had seen Nuo kiss him, and he laid the Baby in their midst. The pretty little child looked up at him with surprise at this solemn beneficence.

She tugged on her mother and said with her American accent, "Mommy, he gave me Baby Jesus. He is so good!"

"Yes, darling. He has so loved the world that He gave His only Son." She had not noticed Jian's gift.

The little girl looked up at Jian, startled and delighted. "He gave me Jesus!" she proclaimed and kissed the figure. The mother hushed her, not unmoved by her baby piety.

Jian was so touched by these words that he barely noticed the snow falling lightly as he stepped outside, and he did not cover his head. Ah, there was a shimmer of light on the steps! He did notice that. Why was it so compelling, why did he love to paint this very likeness on his snow globes? He must add a little more sparkle around the edges next time. And then he laughed. He had not held a brush for years. He walked through the streets with a tear in his eye and a warm heart. Baby Jesus had always been with him, and He was with him still, although his pocket was empty.

The tiny boy moved a miniature figure across the pew.

耶稣

O nce home, he sat at the table he had shared with Nuo and poured a special cup of holiday tea he had been saving. On a whim, he set out a cup for her and, in Western fashion, a Christmas cookie on a holiday plate. Perhaps she would come with Santa down the stovepipe. This thought pleased him. He reached for the candle he had kept for this night and set it on the windowsill to proclaim to the icy world that a light had come to dispel the darkness.

But the darkness could not comprehend it. Neither would the darkness overcome it, though it was a lone flame.

A droplet of melted snow rolled down his forehead, down his nose to the tip, and plopped into his cup. A long, frozen tear waiting to thaw. He began to sob, surprising himself with the sudden depth of his feelings. His country so needed Baby Jesus. How had his beautiful people turned their backs on the Infant? How had some become Herod's men, crushing the bones of new life and destroying the hopes of young men and women in love? And yet so many went to their workbenches in plants and factories and workshops and produced millions of Nativity babies every year. If the West ever abandoned the Infant, the shop in Fulida and many others would close, and then surely the light would go out throughout the world. There would be no voice for the never-born of China.

The ever-born Savior must live.

But what could Jian do against the darkness? No one would look at him and say that his Faith had brought him luck or a greater share in the world's goods. This made him laugh. Only he knew how happy he was, how content. How could he explain it to others? Oh yes, he valued life in the old way, and he, who would have welcomed it many times over, was deprived of parents, siblings, wife, children, son. He had no family before him, none beside him, none after him. The Church would pray for her dead, but there would be no one to light a candle for him. In that moment, he was grateful that he had no dependency on ancestor worship, for surely in all the world there would be no corner and no little altar for him.

He had an inspiration that drew his mind from these glum thoughts back to the feast day. He would make one last globe. How had he not thought of this before? He sprang from his chair to get the supply kit that he was to refresh for a new artist in the studio.

The warm tea and Christmas thoughts had brought a new energy to his fingers. He thought little of his clumsiness.

Jian opened his kit, fussed with the colors, and etched out a scene. The ornament would memorialize both the birth of Jesus and his own death, the death of Zhang Jian. It would speak of his heart's delight. He thought of the little children at Mass and drew the young boy standing next to Baby Jesus. In his hand was a golden heart, on his face was love, in the heart was a wound. The wound dropped petals of plum blossoms that fluttered around the manger. The Babe was also swaddled in the five-petaled blossoms, snug against the winter snow. Renshu and the others would understand that the Baby was swaddled in strength, purity, and the promise of new life, for this was the meaning of the plum blossoms. They would know that Jian had given his heart to this Child. This was enough, even though perhaps they would never know why.

When he finished, Jian cleaned and replaced the brushes. With bread and tea, he toasted the slow rising of the new winter sun. Jian put the globe in the eastern window to catch the light. He prayed the old prayers: "At daybreak we were filled with Your mercy. We rejoiced and were delighted." He lay down happily on his couch and drifted off to a gentle Christmas slumber. He never awakened from his dreams of snowflakes and plum blossoms.

In his hand was a golden heart, on his face
was love, in the heart was a wound.

圣诞花

Renshu visited Jian's apartment in the days after the funeral. He told others that he would go to take care of his old friend's tools and to clean. Secretly he hoped for one thing: to find something there that would speak of Jian. He could not bear to think that a man who had loved so simply the most beautiful of stories, and who had asked for so little in life, and had been deprived of family past and family future, would also be rendered silent by the grave. Jian had taught him so much with his brushes, and Renshu longed for one last word.

He was right to come. For hanging in the window that early morning was the glorious globe of plum blossoms swirling around a golden manger. And in its brightness he glimpsed the power of the Nativity story that reached beyond the grave and touched his Chinese spirit. At once he desired to give his own heart to the Child who promised new life.

He hoped with all his heart that he would meet his friend again. He sat down and closed his eyes and savored the moment. It was good to hope. This was a joy-giving hope. Without any expectation that his worldly life would be improved by this hope, he had hope nonetheless, and it gave him joy!

Renshu now understood the gift that Jian, with his quiet talent, had always extended to him: it was the innocent joy of youth; it was the gift of hope with all its playful freshness. He understood at once that at the center of Western civilization was a baby. Like Jian, the Westerners often carried Him in their pocket. Before, Renshu could not keep track of what was Christian and what was myth. But now he understood why Jian had painted Baby Jesus sometimes poor and sometimes glorious.

And he understood why there were gifts and Santa; angels, kings, and shepherds; camels and snowmen; snowflakes, plum blossoms, and starlight; sheep and oxen and asses; decked-out trains, trolleys, and mantelpieces; sleighs and the improbable Rudolph. He had thought the myths were due to the corruption of exploiting merchants. It had never occurred to him that it was all part of the playful celebration of a heavenly Baby's birthday. It was the kind of celebration a heavenly Child might arrange. It was all joy. China had not honored Him, but the Baby still invited them to celebrate His birthday. Renshu must find a way to tell his countrymen, for they loved festivals.

Renshu stood up and took the globe from its hook. Jian had shown him where his heart was.

He was right to come. For hanging in the window
that early morning was the glorious globe of plum
blossoms swirling around a golden manger.

He looked out the window. He knew he must find one of Jian's priests who would teach him the reasons for his hope. He would not be left behind. He must find the gateway to the nursery of Heaven, for there he would meet his friend and, with him, the Hope of all the world.

爱	love
喜悦	joy
宁静	peaceful
同情	sympathy
和谐	harmonious
美	beauty
圣诞	Christmas
祷告	prayer
星	star
儿童	child
记忆	memory
耶稣	Jesus
圣诞花	Christmas blossoms

ABOUT THE
AUTHOR

Priscilla Smith McCaffrey is one of nine daughters of John and Mary Smith who did not live on Main Street, USA. (There is one brother.) She graduated from Thomas Aquinas College and later worked as research assistant to Fr. John Hardon, S.J., while studying Sacred Doctrine at St. John's University in New York. She taught in Catholic schools and was saved from law school when she married writer and publisher Roger McCaffrey and then homeschooled their four children. She is blissful when in the garden or laughing with her grandchildren, who see life from a Pooh kind of view. ("I will be much bigger when I put away this puzzle.") Meet her at CatholicMediaApostolate.com on two podcasts, where she talks about subjects of interest to homeschoolers and Catholic seniors.

ABOUT THE ILLUSTRATOR

Gwyneth Thompson-Briggs is a painter in the perennial tradition of Western sacred art. Her work decorates churches, schools, and homes throughout the Americas and Europe. In 2019, she founded the Catholic Artists Directory to connect patrons and artists for a new Renaissance of beauty. She lives in Saint Louis with her husband and three small children. You can view her art at GwynethThompsonBriggs.com.

ABOUT
SOPHIA INSTITUTE

Sophia Institute is a nonprofit institution that seeks to nurture the spiritual, moral, and cultural life of souls and to spread the gospel of Christ in conformity with the authentic teachings of the Roman Catholic Church.

Sophia Institute Press fulfills this mission by offering translations, reprints, and new publications that afford readers a rich source of the enduring wisdom of mankind.

Sophia Institute also operates the popular online resource CatholicExchange.com. *Catholic Exchange* provides world news from a Catholic perspective as well as daily devotionals and articles that will help readers to grow in holiness and live a life consistent with the teachings of the Church.

In 2013, Sophia Institute launched Sophia Institute for Teachers to renew and rebuild Catholic culture through service to Catholic education. With the goal of nurturing the spiritual, moral, and cultural life of souls, and an abiding respect for the role and work of teachers, we strive to provide materials and programs that are at once enlightening to the mind and ennobling to the heart; faithful and complete, as well as useful and practical.

Sophia Institute gratefully recognizes the Solidarity Association for preserving and encouraging the growth of our apostolate over the course of many years. Without their generous and timely support, this book would not be in your hands.

www.SophiaInstitute.com
www.CatholicExchange.com
www.SophiaInstituteforTeachers.org

Sophia Institute Press® is a registered trademark of Sophia Institute. Sophia Institute is a tax-exempt institution as defined by the Internal Revenue Code, Section 501(c)(3). Tax ID 22-2548708.